Glamour! * Talent!

* Stardom! *

* Fame and fortune *
could be one step away!

* Welcome to *

**Fame School**

For another fix of

read

Reach for the Stars
Secret Ambition
Rivals!
Tara's Triumph
Lucky Break
Solo Star
Christmas Stars
Pop Diva
Battle of the Bands

# Fame School

## Rising Star

## Cindy Jefferies

USBORNE

Thanks to John Acock, Natalie Powers,
Seb, Ben, Joss and George of Stitch and
Yellow Shark Studios in Cheltenham.

For my daughter Rebecca, with much love

First published in 2005 by Usborne Publishing Ltd., Usborne House,
83-85 Saffron Hill, London EC1N 8RT, England. www.usborne.com

This is a work of fiction. The characters, incidents, and dialogues are products of the
author's imagination and are not to be construed as real. Any resemblance to actual events
or persons, living or dead, is entirely coincidental.

A CIP catalogue record for this book is available from the British Library.

JFMAMJJASO D/07

ISBN 9780746061183

Printed in Great Britain.

# 1 New School

The limousine swished past the wrought-iron gates and up the drive. It drew to a halt with a crunch of gravel outside the impressive front entrance. Chloe got out to the cheers of her fans, who had waited all day to see their favourite pop star.

Well, it was a nice thought. But today's reality wasn't quite as exciting as Chloe's daydream. There *were* plenty of cool cars arriving at Rockley Park School, but Chloe's family owned a rather old Vauxhall with a cracked bumper, not a limousine. Never mind. One day the dream might come true. After all, this was only Chloe's first day at her new school. Winning a scholarship to this very special place *might* be the first step to pop stardom. Because, as well as all the usual lessons, this school taught everything that a singer needed to know!

Rockley Park was a school for aspiring pop stars, songwriters and musicians. It was full of students who were really talented and determined to get to the top. Here, Chloe would get all the voice training she needed, as well as learning how to dance, record her own songs, and all the technical stuff she would need for a career in the music industry.

Chloe peered out of the car. Her dad had followed the signs, and pulled up outside a new building at the back of beautiful old Rockley Park House. This was Paddock House, where all the year seven and year eight girls slept. A long row of windows looked out over the car park and the fields beyond. One of those windows might be Chloe's room...

"Well," said Mum. "We're here." Chloe's little brother Ben had been asleep, but as Chloe opened the door and scrambled out, he woke up.

"Me too," he demanded, and Chloe leaned in to

undo his seat harness.

"Don't let him run off," Mum warned. "You know what he's like." But Ben was still too sleepy to run anywhere. He stuck his thumb in his mouth and watched some people nearby unloading a large trunk from the back of a four-wheel-drive. Chloe wished she could have a trunk, but they were far too expensive – her family just couldn't afford one. Dad opened the boot and took out the shabby suitcase they'd packed Chloe's belongings in. Chloe grabbed two full carrier bags and Mum picked up Ben.

Chloe had been waiting impatiently for this day ever since she'd found out that she'd won a scholarship. But now she'd arrived she had mixed feelings. Thank goodness Danny James, a drummer from her old school, had won a place as well. At least there would be *one* face here she would recognize.

"Excited?" asked Dad. Chloe nodded, but it certainly wasn't just excitement she was feeling. There was a whole cloud of butterflies fluttering about in her stomach and a lot of unanswered questions in her head. Would she be homesick? Would she be able to make friends? Would she find the school work too difficult? Most important of all, was she a good enough singer to make it to the top?

A woman with dark, curly hair was at the front door.

"Welcome to Paddock House," she said, shaking hands with Chloe and her parents. "You are…?" she asked Chloe cheerfully.

"Chloe Tompkins."

"Right, Chloe. I'm Mrs. Pinto, your housemistress. Any problems or worries, you come to me, and if you don't want to do that Mrs. O'Flannery over in the health centre will sort you out." She checked the list she was holding. "Now, your room is on the first floor, at the end of the corridor. There will be four of you in there, all year sevens, of course. Come along. I'll show you the way."

Chloe's family all traipsed along behind Mrs. Pinto.

It was chaotic in the house. There were lots of fire doors that were stiff to open, and the stairs and corridors were full of other girls and their parents, all loaded with belongings, trying to squeeze past each other. You could tell the new girls easily. They were the ones that looked lost, with harassed parents attached. The older girls were much more lively. They greeted each other with squeals of delight and got in the way of everyone else by hugging each other enthusiastically.

"*Do* move out of the way, girls," Mrs. Pinto told a group of four chattering together excitedly. "Go and get some tea if you've unpacked. You can catch up with all your news in the dining room."

Eventually, Mrs. Pinto opened yet another door and stood aside to let Chloe and her family in.

"Here you are," she said. "It looks as if the two beds by the window have already been taken, so choose which one you'd like on the other side and get settled in. Tea is in the dining room in the main house when you're ready. I usually suggest that parents say goodbye here," she said to Chloe's mum. "Do come into the kitchen downstairs for a cup of tea with the rest of the parents, though, before you head for home. It's on the right by the front door."

"Do you want us to help you unpack?" asked Chloe's mum once Mrs. Pinto had gone.

"No, thanks," said Chloe.

Dad could see how she felt. "Come on," he said to his wife, who was hovering around, looking helpless. "Chloe needs to sort herself out. I expect her new roommates will be back soon. Hey! Don't do that," he added, going over to Ben. Chloe's little brother was jumping up and down on one of the beds by the window. "That belongs to some other famous pop star."

"Dad! No one here will be famous for years and years," Chloe said.

They all hugged each other and Mum kept telling Chloe to be sure to ask if she needed help, to eat sensibly, to put her clothes away neatly...until Dad practically had to *drag* her out.

"Bye!" she said again at the door. "Don't lose that mobile phone, will you? Call us tomorrow so we know how you're getting on and we'll see you in three weeks' time. Take care, now!"

Then they were gone.

Chloe went to look out of the window. There were sheep in a nearby field, and some rooks were cawing in a group of tall trees. It was a very different view from the one at home, which was all houses and small gardens. She went and sat down on one of the available beds, the one furthest from the door, and swung her legs, trying to work out how she felt. A bit of her wished she was in the car with her family, going back home, but mostly she was thinking about her new life. She had a fantastic chance now, and she couldn't wait to get on with her singing lessons, but first of all, she had to meet her roommates.

A tall, thin girl had appeared in the doorway, with a smart, black, leather bag over her shoulder. Following her was a man in overalls pushing an ancient, battered trunk on a trolley.

"Put it there," the girl told him regally, pointing to the floor by the only spare bed. He dumped the trunk on the floor and disappeared. She didn't seem to have her parents with her.

# Rising Star

The girl stared at Chloe for a moment and Chloe's heart sank. Of all the people to be sharing with! This was the girl who had been so horrible to Chloe on audition day. Tara! Chloe would have known her disapproving face anywhere. What a rotten start to her new life. Sharing with Tara was going to be awful!

# 2 Friends

"Hi," drawled Tara, looking away. She didn't seem to have recognized Chloe, but it was plain she wasn't interested in being friendly.

"Hi," Chloe muttered in reply and picked up one of her carrier bags. She was just about to empty it onto the bed when two more girls arrived, the ones who had already taken the best beds. Chloe glanced up at them and hastily looked away again. Oh no! This was terrible. How could she possibly make friends with these two? They were Pop 'n' Lolly, the famous model twins who had featured in Chloe's magazine last month!

Chloe had passed Pop 'n' Lolly on the stairs on audition day and had wondered what they were doing at Rockley Park. It hadn't occurred to her that they might have been there for an audition too. Chloe knew Pop and Lolly were the same age as her. She'd read loads about them in her magazine, but it hadn't said they were coming to Rockley Park. How wrong had Chloe been to tell her dad that no one here would be famous for years. How awful if she and Danny turned out to be the only ordinary people at this school.

Pop and Lolly were greeting Tara as an old friend. Chloe swallowed nervously. It was getting worse. She could see how it was going to be. It would be three against one. Perhaps if they were all horrible to her she could ask to be moved to a different room.

Chloe shook the contents of her carrier bag onto the bed and started sorting it out. Those twins needn't think she would suck up to them because they were famous. Just because she had plastic bags and shabby suitcases, it didn't mean she wasn't as good as them!

She stuck out her chin defiantly and picked up some photographs. One, in a frame, was of her and her best friend Jess, pretending to be pop singers. Chloe had thought it was a great picture when she was at home. Now, she was afraid these girls would think it was stupid, and laugh at her.

The other picture, of her and Ben, was less embarrassing. She propped it up against the lamp on her bedside table and tried to stop wishing she was at home.

"Hi!"

Chloe was too busy being determined not to feel homesick to realize that one of the twins was talking to her.

"Hi," the girl said again, coming over to Chloe's side of the room. Chloe looked up and the photo of her and Ben chose that moment to slide off the table and onto the floor. "I'll get it!" the girl offered. Chloe didn't know if it was Pop or Lolly.

While the famous twin was crouching on the floor, reaching for the photograph, Chloe looked at her curiously. It was odd, seeing someone so well known scrabbling about on the floor by your bed. It made

Chloe feel a bit as if she were on the big wheel at a fair – it was like that moment, just before you swoosh down, when your stomach isn't quite sure how it feels.

The girl grabbed the photo and got up, flicking her long, shiny, black hair behind her shoulders. Even close up she was amazingly beautiful, with her almond eyes and flawless, coffee-coloured complexion. She made Chloe feel terribly plain and dull.

"Here it is! Oh! Is that you with your little brother?" She plonked herself down on the bed by Chloe. "Isn't he gorgeous... What's his name?"

"Ben," said Chloe, furious with herself for feeling so shy.

"I'm Poppy by the way, but everyone calls me Pop. My face is fatter than my sister's and she has a little mole on her cheek. That's how you tell us apart!"

"I'm Chloe," said Chloe, wondering if the other twin chattered as much as this one.

"Well, hi Chloe! Pleased to meet you," Pop said. "Hey, Lol!" she called to her sister. "Come over here!" In a moment, the other twin was peering at the picture of Ben sitting on Chloe's lap in the garden. "This is Chloe," Pop introduced them. "Chloe, this is my crazy twin sister Polly, known as Lolly 'cos that was the only way I could say her name when I was little!"

"Ah, he's so sweet," said Lolly, shoving Chloe's belongings aside and sitting down too.

"Not always," said Chloe.

"I wish *I* had a little brother. He can't be worse than Lolly," Pop told her. "She's *so* annoying sometimes."

"Only when you're annoying *me,*" Lolly replied.

"See what I mean?" said Pop. "She's impossible!"

"Don't tell Chloe how horrible we are, Pop, or she won't want to be friends," said Lolly mildly. She picked up the other photograph. "Who's this?"

Chloe blushed. "My friend Jess and me."

"She looks nice," Lolly commented and put the picture down. Pop giggled and grinned at Chloe. "We've got loads of pictures like that. We love dressing up too!"

Chloe couldn't believe what was happening. Pop and Lolly, the famous twins, were being friendly.

Perhaps things *would* be all right after all.

"Hey, Tara," Lolly called over. "Come and look at this sweet picture of Chloe's brother." Without turning round, Tara muttered something that Chloe couldn't catch.

Lolly shrugged. "Pay no attention to Tara," she whispered in Chloe's ear. "She's a bit weird but she's all right once you get used to her. Her mother's a fashion journalist, and sometimes we've been dragged to the same parties by our parents."

"Tea!" said Pop. "That's what I want. Come on. I'm starved!" So the three of them left Tara unpacking her trunk and headed over to the main house.

It was fun being with Pop and Lolly. Loads of people stared at the twins. They were so famous almost everyone recognized them.

"Just ignore them," Lolly told Chloe. But Chloe found herself starting to giggle.

"They all know who *you* are," she muttered to Pop. "But they must be wondering who I am!"

"You're the next big thing!" said Pop firmly.

"Absolutely!" agreed Lolly, pulling Chloe's arm

through hers. "What have you come to Rockley Park to study?"

"Singing," said Chloe.

"Like us! So you're the next pop diva, then," Pop said with a grin. "You must be, because I say so. And I'm *never* wrong," she added grandly.

"We've come to study here because our agent said we ought to have another string to our bow," Lolly told Chloe.

"After all, modelling work doesn't last for ever!" said Pop. "Sooner or later, magazines will want new faces."

Chloe couldn't imagine the twins *ever* being turned down for a modelling job, but before she could say so, she caught sight of another face she recognized. "There's Danny!" she said excitedly. "He was at my last school."

"He looks nice," Lolly said. "Let's go and sit with him. Is he a singer too?"

"No," Chloe explained. "He's a drummer."

"Wow! I've never met a proper drummer before," said Pop.

# Rising Star

"Come on, then," Chloe urged the twins. "I'll introduce you."

The day was turning out to be much better than Chloe had imagined. Pop and Lolly were more than making up for having to share with Tara. It was going to be such fun being friends with them.

# 3 Rising Stars

Danny was sitting by himself at a small yellow table.

"Save me a seat," said Lolly, "while I grab some drinks."

"I'll get food," said Pop. "You'll have to save us *two* seats, Chloe!"

Chloe and Danny grinned at each other. Although she wasn't homesick at all now, it was great to see Danny's familiar face. "You got here all right, then?" she said.

"Yeah, I just arrived. I haven't missed the welcome meeting, have I?"

"No," Chloe reassured him. "Don't worry, we haven't had it yet."

Danny looked over at the food queue. "I see you've made friends already."

"I'm sharing a room with them," said Chloe. "Have you got nice roommates?"

"Dunno," Danny said with a shrug. "I just dropped my bag off and came straight over here. This place is a bit different from Beacon Comp," he added. "It's more like a hotel than a school."

He was right. All the walls were newly painted, the floors were polished, and the beautiful plasterwork on the dining-room ceiling was picked out in blue and gold. But the food bar was the same as at Beacon Comprehensive, and there were enough students talking loudly round the plastic tables to remind Chloe that she really was at school.

"Here you go!" Pop and Lolly dumped a couple of trays onto the table and sat down either side of Chloe.

"Help yourselves," added Lolly, doling out some plates and pushing a mug of tea and some squash in Chloe's direction. "I didn't know what you like to drink," she added. "Cake?" she offered Danny. "Go on. It looks really good! We got plenty."

"Okay. Thanks." Danny took a piece of chocolate cake. "Have you seen a timetable yet?" he asked Chloe. She shook her head, munching cake.

"I think they're up in the hall," Lolly told him.

"Oh, right. I'll go and have a look," Danny said, finishing his cake and getting up. "I want to see when my first drum lesson is. See you later. Nice to meet you," he added to the twins awkwardly.

"Is he always so keen on lessons?" Pop asked, watching Danny weave his way between the tables and out of the room.

"Just drum lessons, I think," Chloe said.

"There's nothing wrong with liking lessons," Lolly said.

Pop laughed. "It's all right for you!" she told her sister. "You're good at them! Come on," she added. "The meeting will be starting any minute. We'd better go!"

There was no need to follow the signs. The girls tagged on to the cluster of new students filing into the theatre. There were only about twenty-five year sevens including Chloe and the twins. In Chloe's last school there had been six year-seven classes, but here there would probably only be one. Looking round and seeing how few pupils there were at this school, Chloe realized just how lucky she had been to get her place at Rockley Park.

The theatre was very new and modern. The tiered seating looked comfortable, and the bank of lights over the stage seemed very professional. Chloe stared at the stage in excitement. One day soon, she would be performing right there. She couldn't wait!

Mrs. Sharkey, the Principal, walked onto the stage and the buzz of excited voices quietened down.

"Welcome to Rockley Park," she said, smiling at everyone. "I hope you've enjoyed your tea and are beginning to feel at home. Because we only have room for two hundred students here, we are more like a family than a school. But that doesn't mean we don't expect you to work hard! The teachers will give you grades for all the usual subjects, like any other school. However," she paused, "they will also be grading you for your musical endeavours. Every music lesson and every piece of creative work will be assessed, and your progress noted in points. You will also perform at regular school concerts, where your fellow students, as the audience, will have the chance to award you points as well. These points will be added up over each term and, at the end of the school year, the best students will be chosen by the teachers to perform at a special concert called Rising Stars."

*I'm going to be a Rising Star,* Chloe told herself excitedly. *As soon as I possibly can!*

But Mrs. Sharkey hadn't finished. "The annual Rising Stars concert is important because it is shown on local television, and is watched with great interest by A&R people."

A buzz of excited voices ran round the auditorium. Chloe had heard of A&R, though she didn't know what it stood for, but *television*! She couldn't wait to text Jess. And how proud her parents would be, if only she could do it! She must work hard at her singing lessons and perform really well at every concert to get loads of these Rising Stars points.

"The first school concert will be the Christmas one, at the end of term, so you only have a few weeks to practise."

Chloe was too excited about the concert to take in the rest of the talk, so she was glad when Mrs. Sharkey said, "You can make your way back to your houses now. Pick up your timetables in the hall, and don't forget to look on the noticeboard for the time of your first individual lessons. Good luck, everyone. I hope you all enjoy your time at Rockley Park School."

Everyone was chattering noisily as they pushed out of the theatre.

"What are A&R people?" Chloe quickly asked Lolly.

"It's short for Artistes and Repertoire. They're talent scouts," Lolly said. "They work for recording companies. So it's really cool if one spots you."

"Wow!" Chloe's head was full of hopes and plans for her performance in the first concert. Should she sing her audition song or would her singing teacher help her to choose a new one?

"Remember audition day?" said Pop as they

wandered through the main hall. "And how scared we all were?"

"I can't imagine *you* were scared," said Chloe, remembering how she'd seen the twins coming confidently down the stairs. "After all, there are two of you, and you're already so famous."

"Not for singing though," said Pop. "I was really worried that only one of us might get in. I don't know *what* we'd have done if that had happened."

"Look, Chloe! Your singing lesson is first thing tomorrow!" said Lolly, reading from a list on the board. "It's before registration, and ours is on Tuesday."

They picked up a year-seven timetable each, and skimmed through them on the way to their room.

"Dance, three periods a week," said Pop approvingly. "Songwriting! One period a week. I don't think I'll be much good at that."

"Music technology," read Chloe. She remembered the recording studio that had been so fascinating during her guided tour on audition day. "That sounds good."

It was fun, unpacking together, in spite of Tara's

grumpy remarks. Chloe discovered that Pop and Lolly had each brought a favourite soft toy. And when even Tara propped an ancient teddy on her pillow, Chloe felt able to reveal her own favourite, a monkey that her granny had given her years ago. When Mrs. Pinto, their housemistress, came to say goodnight, they were still all giggling and laughing.

"Settle down now, girls," she said. "The bell will go at seven in the morning, and you don't want to be tired on your first day."

She turned off their light, and Chloe listened to her footsteps going down the corridor to the next room. So much had happened since she'd arrived. She still couldn't believe that the famous Pop and Lolly were sleeping in the same room as her. But the three of them got on so well, Chloe was sure they would be best friends. Somehow, it felt as if they'd known each other for ages. She was bubbling with excitement, too, at the thought of her first singing lesson in the morning. At last, all her dreams of being taken seriously as a singer were about to come true.

# 4 Singing Lesson

By seven thirty the next morning, they were in the dining room, choosing their breakfast. They'd just sat down when Danny turned up.

"Can we sit with you?" he asked. A ginger-haired boy was with him. The boy's amazing orange hair was long and curly and he had a grin like a clown.

"Sure," said the twins together, and Chloe gave Danny a smile.

"Chloe's friend, Danny," Lolly explained to Tara, who was sitting with them.

"This is Marmaduke. We're sharing a room," Danny said as they both sat down.

"Marmaduke!" That was Tara. "What a ridiculous

name." For someone who looked so sophisticated she could be awfully rude.

"Actually, I'm usually called..."

"With your silly orange hair, you should be called Marmalade!"

Chloe caught her breath. It was a brilliant nickname, but it was cruel of Tara to suggest it. Maybe he was really sensitive about his hair. Some people were. But she needn't have worried. Marmaduke burst into laughter and his curly hair flopped about like a mop.

"Well done! Mind you, you had my real name to help you," he said. "Most people think up the nickname Marmalade before they know what I'm really called. So you weren't *that* clever. I use it as my stage name. Marmalade Stamp, delighted to meet you!"

He tried to shake her hand in a jokey manner, but she folded her arms and glared at him. Chloe was most impressed that he'd defused Tara's nastiness, and made her feel silly instead.

Marmalade shrugged and shook hands with

# Singing Lesson

everyone else instead. All the time his hair was bobbing and flopping all over the place.

"Delighted," he kept saying. It sounded so old fashioned, and really funny. But Chloe kept looking at the clock, and was becoming rather nervous.

"I must go," she said, jumping up from her seat and leaving her breakfast unfinished. "I'll see you later. I've got my singing lesson now." The butterflies were back, fluttering about in her stomach.

She hadn't forgotten how to get to Mr. Player's room. But she hesitated outside. The last time she'd been here was audition day. In some ways, that day had been a disaster, but in spite of messing up the audition, she had her scholarship place, and here she was, all set to be a proper singer. This was the beginning of the Big Chance she had waited so long for. She *must* make the most of it. She took a deep breath, tapped at the door and walked in.

Mr. Player had long fair hair which fell over his very blue eyes. He was about her parents' age, and still really good looking. He had been a pop singer

31

himself some years ago, but he'd given up performing to be a teacher. Chloe's mum had some of his CDs at home and had dug them out to show Chloe. It had been weird to see her teacher's face on the cover of a CD!

"Well, Chloe," said Mr. Player. "It's nice to see you again. Are you all settled in?"

Chloe nodded. "Yes, thank you."

"Can you give me a moment to read your notes?"

Chloe looked round the room while she waited for him to read the notes he had in a folder. She remembered the grand piano, and the pianist, Mrs. Jones. Mrs. Jones looked up from a book she was reading and gave Chloe a friendly smile.

The room was beautiful. It was quite large, with tall windows and a high ceiling. A thick, green carpet covered most of the polished floorboards, and at the end of the room a full-length mirror stood next to a water cooler. Near the piano was a shelf with an expensive-looking stereo system on it.

"Your notes say that you haven't had any voice

training before," said Mr. Player. "Don't worry!" he added, seeing the expression on her face. "It's not important. And it means you won't be able to complain that I'm not as good as your last teacher!" He smiled. He was trying to put her at ease. Chloe relaxed a bit and smiled back.

"Right. There are a couple of things before we start. Over there, you've probably noticed the water cooler. Some people like to have a drink with them when they sing and others don't. I'm happy either way. All I ask is that if you do, you pour the water at the beginning of the lesson and let it come up to room temperature before you drink it. It's better for your voice that way."

Chloe hesitated. She didn't know whether she would need a drink or not.

"I tell you what," Mr. Player said, seeing her uncertainty. "Why don't you go and get some anyway? It won't matter if you don't drink it." So Chloe went over to the water cooler and filled a paper cup.

"There's a mat here," he showed her. "Don't put it

straight onto the piano or Mrs. Jones will tell us off!" Mrs. Jones smiled at Chloe again, and Chloe smiled nervously back.

"Let's do some humming," said Mr. Player. "It's important to warm up your voice before you use it, and humming is a good exercise to start with." He nodded to Mrs. Jones and she played a chord on the piano. "I'll hum with you."

Together they hummed up and down, a few notes at a time. Chloe started enjoying herself. It was fun. Every now and then she carried on alone while Mr. Player gave her advice. "Relax. Keep your shoulders down. That's good."

By the time they stopped humming, Chloe's lips were buzzing. She took a sip of water, feeling very grown up and professional.

"Okay. Now let's do some scales so I can remind myself of your range. No pressure, just sing each note as Mrs. Jones plays it. Don't strain your voice. If there are any notes you can't reach, just leave them out."

Well, that didn't sound too difficult. Chloe had done

that before. She lah lah'd her way up the scales as Mrs. Jones played them on the piano. She went quite a long way but eventually she had to stop.

Mr. Player picked up a pen and marked the notes in her folder where it lay on top of the piano.

"Well done!" he said. "You're singing well up the scale. Now let's try going down."

So they did, and Mr. Player was even more pleased. "Yes," he said, marking her notes again. "Most impressive. You do have a remarkable range, and you're hitting the notes quite accurately. Can you read music?"

Chloe shook her head worriedly. "No."

"It doesn't matter," he assured her. "I only wondered. Let's see how accurate you are when we play random notes... Yes, good. That's very good," he went on as the notes came in any order for her to sing.

Chloe smiled. This was proving easier than she'd thought, but Mr. Player wasn't smiling any more. In fact, he looked a bit concerned.

"There's just one thing," he said. "Why are you only using your throat to sing?"

Chloe frowned. Didn't everyone use their throat? What else was she supposed to use?

But it wasn't a joke. From the expression on his face, it was obvious that Mr. Player thought she was doing something very wrong indeed!

# 5 Chloe has a Problem

"Maybe you're singing from your throat because you're nervous," Mr. Player suggested to Chloe. "But you can't get enough power singing this way. You need to be able to sing much more loudly for me. *Are* you feeling nervous?"

"A bit," she admitted. But she hadn't been while she'd been singing. She'd got over her nervousness and had been enjoying the humming and scales. She was only nervous now because Mr. Player was unhappy with how she was singing.

"Let's try a nursery rhyme," he suggested. "Maybe you've been worrying too much about getting the pitch right. Do you know *Baa Baa Black Sheep*? Let's hear it good and loud. Pretend you're singing it to a little boy all the way down there by the mirror."

Chloe looked at the mirror. She tried to imagine singing to Ben, but if he were there he'd come racing up the room and throw his arms round her knees. Now she was nervous *and* homesick!

Mr. Player smiled encouragingly. "Come on, Chloe. Don't worry about being in tune. Just give me some volume."

Now, volume hadn't been Chloe's thing since she was eight years old and her primary school teacher hadn't let her sing in the choir. She'd said Chloe's voice didn't fit in with the rest of the children's voices. In a way, the teacher had been right. Chloe's voice didn't fit, but only because it had been so powerful, and so much louder than all the others. She hadn't sung out of tune.

At home, it was almost as bad. Once Ben had been born, Chloe couldn't sing loudly because of disturbing her baby brother. Over the years, she'd got out of the habit of singing in anything much more than a whisper. Had she forgotten how to do it?

"Come on, Chloe," urged Mr. Player. "Give it all you've got!"

She tried but he winced.

"Now you're shouting," he complained. "And even your shout isn't very loud."

"Sorry," Chloe mumbled. This was terrible. How could she make her voice louder? Her first voice lesson was going dreadfully.

"It's all right," Mr. Player said. "Don't panic. But you'll have to work on this. You're going to need power as well as your excellent range to sing professionally. Even using a microphone, to get real expression into a song you need to be able to sing quietly, *and* power away as well." Chloe nodded miserably.

"The school day is about to start," he said, looking at his watch. "And we haven't got through as much as I'd hoped. Never mind. Don't you *ever* sing loudly?"

Chloe shook her head. "I've always just sung in my room because my teacher at primary school, Mrs. Pendle, said my voice didn't suit the choir. And I have to keep quiet because of my little brother," she explained.

Mr. Player shook his head. "Poor you! Well, some people instinctively use their tummy muscles when they sing, but you're only singing from your throat. Don't worry. You'll get it. You have to learn to use your tummy muscles to push the air out of your lungs. That's your problem. I should think being told to sing quietly all the time hasn't helped, but here you'll be able to sing as loudly as you like! And that's what I'm here for, to help iron out any problems. Once we've got you over this hurdle, we can get on with more exciting things." He smiled at her.

"The most important thing is that you don't strain your voice by trying too hard. Don't overdo it. I just want you to think about where the sound comes from. It should come from deep inside you. If you put your hand on your tummy while you sing, you should be able to feel your muscles working. All right?"

Chloe nodded uncertainly.

There was a knock on the door and Mr. Player closed Chloe's file. "Don't worry," he said. "It's early days. I'll see you later in the week."

Chloe had to rush to get back for registration at Paddock House. She felt dreadful. Instead of being on the way to fame, she felt as if she was on her way to disaster!

She had worked so hard to convince her parents that singing was what she really wanted to do. After the tussle to get them to agree to her trying for a place, and the nail-biting audition, she had finally got to Rockley Park School, only to find that she couldn't sing properly.

Mr. Player had told her not to worry, but how could she *not* worry? What if she couldn't get her voice right in time to sing in the concert? Chloe desperately wanted those Rising Star points, but they felt a million miles away now. Then, an even worse thought crept into her mind. What if she *never* got her voice right? No, that was too terrifying to contemplate.

Ambition had got Chloe to Rockley Park, that and determination. She took a deep breath and decided that she *would* sing brilliantly at the concert, come what may. It was early days. She would find a way.

Maybe she'd be able to pick up some tips from her friends before the next lesson. It wasn't a good idea to panic. So she pushed all her secret fears as far away as possible, into a dark corner of her mind, and went to join the others for registration.

"How did you get on?" Pop asked, sitting at her desk.

"It was a bit disappointing," said Chloe, not wanting to admit to being a total failure. "I wanted to ask about a song for the concert but Mr. Player was going on about me not using the right muscles when I sing."

"What are you doing at this school if you can't sing properly?" said Tara.

"Take no notice," Pop told Chloe, glaring at Tara. "Tara is a bass player. Singing is a sideline for her. She hasn't a clue what she's talking about."

"Don't worry," added Lolly. "It's only your first lesson. The concert isn't for ages. You've got plenty of time to choose a song and I'm sure Mr. Player will get you sorted out."

"He might not," said Tara. Pop scowled at her but she carried on regardless. "If you can't sing properly," she said nastily. "You'll *never* be a Rising Star!"

# 6 A Disappointing Week

Somehow, Chloe had to swallow the disappointment of her first singing lesson, and concentrate on the rest of the school day. There was a full timetable of ordinary lessons, as well as all the extra ones too. After tea, there was supervised homework in the homework room at Paddock House, and by bedtime everyone was exhausted.

"*Our* first singing lesson tomorrow!" said Pop as they climbed into bed.

"Judge Jim Henson, Head of the Rock Department, sat in on my first bass lesson!" bragged Tara. "He might write something for me to play at the concert!"

"Pigs might fly!" Pop shot back. Chloe pulled her

duvet up round her ears and closed her eyes. She'd have to get her singing sorted out quickly or the others would be ahead of her with their concert preparations.

But after several voice lessons, Chloe was still no further forward, in spite of the breathing exercises Mr. Player had asked her to do. At one lesson, he even brought a drawing in to show her, with lungs, diaphragm and stomach muscles marked on it.

"Do your breathing exercises again with your hand on your tummy," he told her patiently. She did as she was told, letting her muscles go slack as she breathed in through her nose, and feeling them tighten as she pushed the last puffs of air back out through her mouth.

"That's what should be happening when you sing," he reminded her.

But Chloe was getting frustrated. "I can't do it!" she replied crossly. "I'm too worried about what I'm going to sing at the concert."

Mr. Player folded his arms and leaned against the piano. "Getting your voice sorted out is far more important than thinking of performing," he said. "There will be other concerts...when you've learned to use your voice properly."

Chloe stared at him in horror. "But I *have* to do the concert," she told him. "I can't possibly miss it!"

"Listen to me," he said. "You have the potential to be an excellent singer, but you'll store up trouble for yourself if you try to perform now. Get your technique right first; *then* you can sing in concerts. Now, don't let me hear any more about it."

Chloe stumbled through the rest of her lesson in a daze. Not sing at the concert? She *had* to sing. *Everyone* was performing. She'd die of shame if Mr. Player wouldn't allow her to take part. She could imagine what Tara would say. And what about those precious Rising Stars points?

After the lesson was over, she pushed open the door to the little courtyard nearby. She didn't feel like joining her friends straight away, and this place had been a refuge for her before, when everything had gone wrong on audition day.

## A Disappointing Week

She was moping so much, she didn't see the figure on the bench until she was halfway there. Judge Jim Henson, the Head of Rock, was sitting in his favourite spot, busy working on an old guitar. He looked up, and smiled.

"Well, hello! It's my old friend, Chloe. How'ya doin'?"

She bit her lip. It was no good pretending to Judge Jim, even if she'd wanted to. He'd calmed her down on audition day and sorted out what was wrong. If she was going to talk to anyone, Judge Jim was the best person to confide in.

"I'm not doing very well," she admitted. "But I've been wanting to thank you for helping me to get my place here."

Judge Jim waved his hand dismissively. "You got the place," he said. "Not me. You want to join me here?" he added. "I'm just restringing this old friend of mine. I'd be happy to have some company."

Chloe went to the bench and Judge Jim moved up so there was enough room for her to sit down. He ran his wrinkled hand down the neck of the guitar.

"Had this since I wasn't too much older than you," he said. "I know she's not much to look at now, but she's my oldest friend. When I first earned myself a load of money, I went out and bought all the best guitars of the day, but somehow this old girl has stayed with me through thick and thin."

Chloe took a look at the instrument he was holding. It didn't look anything special. It was scratched and worn, with loads of painted patterns on it, faded now, but once probably really bright. Its old strings lay discarded on the ground in a springy heap.

"Maybe it would be better if *I* played an instrument," Chloe sighed.

"I thought you had your instrument all neat and tidy in your voice box," Judge Jim said. "You don't need to buy strings to get that working properly."

"But I can't get my voice to work at *all*," Chloe said. As she spoke, her voice wobbled, but she was determined not to cry. She had used one of Judge Jim's huge handkerchiefs to mop up her tears once before, and she didn't want him to have to find another.

Chloe explained about her voice getting quieter and quieter instead of more and more powerful like Mr. Player wanted. She told him about her primary school teacher too; whom Mr. Player thought had ruined her confidence.

"And now, if I can't sing properly, Mr. Player says I won't be able to take part in the *concert*!" She stopped short. It was such a dreadful thing to admit.

All the time she was talking, Judge Jim kept working on his guitar. He said nothing while he fitted the last string and tightened it up. At last, he ran his fingers over them and the strings whispered in the silent courtyard.

"You got amplifier problems," he announced at last. "Like my friend here, you need to hook up to your amplifier before you can perform."

"Yes," said Chloe. "And Mr. Player has taught me all about my tummy muscles, but I still can't do it."

"And why would that be?" asked Judge Jim, adjusting the strings.

Chloe shrugged miserably.

"Does a baby need to learn how to use its muscles

before it can cry?" he asked, his brown eyes meeting hers for the first time.

"No," Chloe shook her head. "I suppose not."

"Well, then. You got the voice. You got the amplifier. Your body knows how to use them, but your mind is interfering. You need to calm down. Be easy on yourself. You might not think it, but you got all the time in the world." He smiled.

"Look at my friend here. I can't tell you the number of times I threw her across the room when I was young 'cause I couldn't get her to sound how I wanted. I was like you, child. I was so full of ambition, and sometimes it worked against me. It was always better once I'd calmed down and relaxed. Sometimes, I thought my hands had lost their cunning, and forgotten how to play, but it wasn't that. You can't make music when you're all scrunched up with anger, or with fear."

"But I *must* get my voice working or I won't be able to sing in the *concert*," Chloe protested.

Judge Jim looked deep into her eyes.

"In your life there will be many, many times when

you can't have what you want," he told her. "In this business, as well as needing determination, you sometimes have to learn to let things go. We're artists, and although any art needs hard work, you can't force it. The more you try to force your voice, the more it will resist you. Relax, give your voice a break, and it'll come back."

"But..."

Judge Jim raised his eyebrows, but didn't argue. He stood up and grunted, stooping to pick up the old strings. He slung the guitar over his shoulder and looked at her.

"I have to go give a lesson. You take care now, and be sure to come and see me again soon."

Chloe watched him leave and then kicked miserably at a pebble on the ground.

*He doesn't understand*, she told herself. *He doesn't! I have to do the concert or I'll have to admit to everyone I can't sing, and then I'll die!*

# 7 Fair Weather Friends?

On the way back to Paddock House, Chloe met a group of year-seven boys discussing what they were going to perform at the concert.

"Hey, Chloe!" yelled Toby Bones, a friend of Danny's, and a singer like Chloe. "How're your plans for the concert going?"

Chloe didn't want to stop, but there was no escape. Everyone gathered round, anxious to share what they were doing.

"I can't get my piece right," confessed Toby ruefully. "Every single time I sing, I forget to breathe in the right place!"

"How's the drumming going?" Chloe hastily asked Danny.

"Okay," he said.

"He's too modest," laughed Toby. "His drumming is fantastic. He's sure to get loads of Rising Stars points. No wonder he got a scholarship!"

"You got a scholarship too, didn't you?" Marmalade said to Chloe. "You must be pretty confident about the concert. What are you singing? Is it something I could dance to?"

Chloe edged away from the boys. "That'd be telling," she said, trying to sound upbeat. "Got to go. It's almost homework time."

She hurried away, and once out of sight she leaned against a wall to catch her breath. She still couldn't face going back to the house. Tara would be crowing about how well her bass piece was going, and Pop would insist on demonstrating the dance routine she'd choreographed with Lolly to go with their song.

Chloe decided to text Jess. Maybe that would make her feel a bit better. And then, next weekend when Chloe went home, she and Jess could try to work out what to do.

"*Help! I've lost my voice. Need 2 tlk,*" she texted. Jess's message came back almost at once, but it wasn't what Chloe wanted to hear.

"*Cant tlk if voice lost! See u next satday.*"

Of course Jess didn't understand what a crisis this was, and it was too complicated to explain in a text. Chloe stuffed the mobile back in her pocket. She had never felt so alone in her life. Everyone at Rockley Park would soon know that she wasn't going to be in the concert, and they would *all* want to know why. When they knew, they would despise her.

A cold ribbon of fear ran down her back. They *would* despise her. This school was all about success, not failure. People like Pop and Lolly had spent their entire lives being successes. They'd probably sympathize with her because they were nice people, but Chloe would be isolated, the only one with nothing to say when the concert was being discussed. She would have no one to talk to, and no Rising Stars points to put towards the all-important concert at the end of the school year!

Chloe couldn't wait for the next week to pass so she could go home for half term. Even though this half term was only a weekend, because the term was so short, it would still give her a breather. At school, she seemed to be spending all her time putting off questions about her choice of song for the concert.

"You're being very secretive about your song," Lolly said one evening when they were washing their hair. "Mr. Player must have come up with something really special for you. I can't wait to find out what it is. Are you going to dance as well, or just sing?"

"Just sing," mumbled Chloe unhappily. She hated lying, especially to Lolly, who was such a good friend, but she couldn't bring herself to admit the truth.

At the last singing lesson before half term, Chloe arrived to find some mellow jazz playing on the stereo. Mrs. Jones wasn't at the piano, and Mr. Player didn't have Chloe's file open as usual.

"This is some of my favourite relaxing music," he told her. "Do you like it?"

Chloe let the soothing notes slide over her mind. She'd never listened to jazz before.

"Mmm," she agreed. "It's good."

"Now, come down here." Mr. Player took her to stand in front of the mirror. "Look how tense you are!" He put his hands on her shoulders and pushed them gently down. "That's better. Let the music flow over you. This is our last lesson before half term, and I want to send you home relaxed and happy."

That was impossible, Chloe thought, but she listened politely.

"I don't want you to worry about doing any exercises, or trying to sing. I've just got one bit of fun homework for you to do. Now tell me something. When was the last time you threw up? It's a serious question," he added, seeing the bewildered expression on her face.

"I think it was last winter," Chloe said, trying to remember. "My little brother got a bug and all my family came down with it. Why?"

"Because I want you to try to remember what

happens when you throw up. Find a quiet corner over half term and practise. I don't really want you to be sick, of course! But have a go at acting it out. Make all the horrible noises you did then. It might help if you get a friend to have a go with you. Have a laugh doing it, but try to reproduce that powerful feeling. Sometimes, doing that helps singers to learn how to project their voices."

Chloe sighed. This wasn't how she had imagined singing lessons at Rockley Park would be. She should be learning how to breathe in the right places, and how to give real feeling to the words she sang, not having to practise being sick! It would have been funny if it weren't so awful.

Mr. Player stopped the music. "Do you have a personal CD player?" he asked.

"Yes."

"Well take this," he said, handing her the jazz CD, "and play it over half term. If you feel like humming along to it, fine. But don't force it. One day you'll unlock that fantastic voice of yours, and then all your worries will fade away to nothing. Have a great half term."

Chloe put the CD in her bag. She knew he was trying to be kind, but it was obvious that she was getting nowhere.

At long last, Friday came. Chloe was in the homework room, asking Lolly about their English homework when Danny arrived with his weekend bag, ready for a lift home with Chloe's parents.

"You're not in the concert!" he said to Chloe with concern, slinging his bag down on her desk. In his hand, he had a copy of the concert programme that had just been printed.

*Oh no!* thought Chloe. *I forgot all about the programme.*

"What?" Pop squeaked. She stared at Danny. "Whatever do you mean? Of course she's in the concert! I've been trying for ages to get her to tell me the song..." She looked over at Chloe. "She said she..."

"Is everything all right?" asked Lolly.

Chloe looked desperately from one of her friends to the other, not knowing what to say.

"I...didn't..." she said, trying to think of something, *anything,* to make it not so bad. Now, she could see it might have been better if she'd been honest with them. But it was too late.

Of course, Tara chose that very moment to arrive.

"Your parents are here," she said. "In their beaten-up old car." She waved the programme in Chloe's face. "Don't suppose you'll be coming back after half term, will you?" she added spitefully. "Oh?" she said, with a smirk, seeing the twins' astonished faces. "Didn't she tell her *best friends* that she's not good enough to be in the concert? Well, there you are. *I* knew she'd never hack it!"

# 8 Home for the Weekend

"How's the singing going?" Dad asked when they were in the car.

"Fine," Chloe said, as cheerfully as she was able. Danny looked at her in surprise.

"What about the con..." Chloe gave him a murderous look and he fell silent. After a few moments he said, "Do you know, I have to learn things called rudiments."

"What are they?" asked Chloe's mum.

"They're all sorts of different rhythms I have to know. They have amazing names, like paradiddle, flam and ruff."

"Goodness."

"They get their names from knitting patterns," Danny added.

Chloe's mum turned round in her seat and stared at him. "Do they?" she said. "How very odd."

"They don't really," he admitted. "That was just something my friend Marmalade told me. He said his granny mutters words like that when she's knitting."

Chloe's mum laughed. "It sounds as if you have lots of fun at this new school of yours," she said. "I'm quite envious."

Danny looked at Chloe and she smiled at him gratefully.

"Thanks," she whispered as her mum turned away. He shrugged.

"It's okay."

It was great to be home. Ben came and bounced on Chloe's bed to wake her the next morning, and she tickled him until he squealed. He was too little to understand all the complications of her life. He didn't care what went on at Rockley Park School. He was simply happy to have his big sister home again, and thought she was perfect the way she was.

Later on, Jess came round to see Chloe. Chloe had been so looking forward to confiding in her oldest friend, but Jess only wanted to hear about the famous people Chloe had met. She didn't seem to realize how much her friend needed to talk.

"If I give you last month's magazine, will you get Pop 'n' Lolly's autographs for me?" Jess pleaded. "They can sign beside the pictures of themselves. It'll be really cool to take that to school. Everyone will be *so* jealous!" She settled herself more comfortably on Chloe's bed. "Who else do you know?"

"*Jess!*"

"What?"

Chloe looked at her friend miserably. "I need to talk to you. I've got a *huge* problem." She hesitated, hearing her parents' voices downstairs. "Not here. Let's go for a walk."

While they dawdled into town, Chloe told Jess all her woes.

"It's not *your* fault," Jess told Chloe stoutly. "It's

that Mrs. Pendle. You can blame her."

"But I've still got to find my voice," Chloe said. "What if the teachers at Rockley Park don't want me any more? I wouldn't blame them."

Jess shook her head. "Well *I* would. They're supposed to be teaching you. They can't just give up. *You're* not giving up. Are you?"

"No!" Chloe bit back her tears. Part of her *was* almost tempted to give up the whole idea of being a pop singer. "I'm not giving up. But Mr. Player told me that I can't be in a concert until I can sing properly. And, I really like Pop and Lolly but they won't want to be my friends if I'm a failure."

"Why not?"

"Oh, Jess! Because they're famous. And successful. And they won't want to mix with failures."

"Is that what they said?"

Chloe tried to be fair. "Well, no, but then, they don't know why I'm not in the concert."

"You mean you haven't told them?"

Chloe's face told Jess all she needed to know. "I

couldn't tell them," she mumbled, scuffing a few dry leaves underfoot. "Or Mum and Dad."

"Chloe, you're so *stupid*." Jess told her. "If you don't tell people your problems, they can't help."

"I *am* telling *you*," Chloe said, nearly in tears.

"Yes, but you need to talk to Pop and Lolly to get them on your side. How can they be friends if you don't trust them? It's horrible if a friend doesn't tell you something important."

They walked on in silence for a few minutes, while Chloe digested what Jess had said. Chloe hadn't told Jess immediately when she'd got her place at Rockley Park and that had really hurt poor Jess. Now, Chloe had made the same mistake with her Rockley Park friends.

"Do you think I ought to text them?" she said.

"Good idea," said Jess. "Say you'll explain on Sunday night. Go on. Do it now!" Jess was always so enthusiastic. She was hard to resist. So Chloe dug the mobile out of her bag. After a moment's thought, she sent the text to Lolly. Chloe thought she was the calmest, most understanding of the twins. All Chloe could do now was to keep her fingers crossed for a friendly reply.

It was ages since Chloe and Jess had been shopping together. Chloe had almost forgotten how much fun it could be. They went into the music store and almost immediately Jess found something in the bargain section that made her giggle.

"Look!" she said. Chloe looked. *Jeremy Player, On My Own Tonite,* was the title on the CD. There was a picture of her teacher looking a lot younger, gazing soulfully into the distance. "Do you want to get it?" asked Jess.

"No way!" said Chloe, laughing. It was rather embarrassing to see Mr. Player on such a cheesy CD.

"Who else do you know who might have a CD out?" said Jess. She was like a terrier, sniffing out any hint of celebrity. Chloe told her about Judge Jim Henson.

"Will he be under H or J?" said Jess, riffling through the racks.

"I don't know," Chloe said uncertainly. "He's played guitar with loads of famous people over the years, but I don't know if he ever made any records of his own.

Don't look under pop, Jess. He's a rock musician!"

Jess moved over to rock. "Here!" she said, almost straight away. "*Judge Jim and Friends.*" She waved the case excitedly, and Chloe took it.

It was him! *Her* friend, too. Judge Jim Henson! In the picture, he was sitting on a plain wooden chair with his old guitar, the one he'd been restringing the other day. He was smiling his warm, easy smile, almost as if it were just for her.

"Wow! I don't really like rock music, but even *I've* heard of lots of these people," squealed Jess, grabbing the CD again so she could read the back. "Eric Clapton, The Beatles, Jimi Hendrix – all these people playing with Judge Jim Henson. And you *know* him!" Chloe nodded. It *was* amazing.

Chloe felt renewed determination flood through her. She was almost part of this world. She couldn't bear to fail now that she had a chance to make it as a pop star. She *had* to get her voice working properly. Her ambition was everything to her, *everything*!

In the park, Jess and Chloe tried the throwing-up

exercise that Mr. Player had suggested, but by then they were in a very silly mood, and even Chloe couldn't take it seriously, so they went on the swings instead.

It was good to spend some time away from her troubles, but later on, after Jess had gone home and Ben was in bed, Chloe decided to talk to her mum and dad about her singing problems.

"I'm supposed to sing from *here*," she explained, putting her hands on her tummy to show them. "And when I do the breathing exercises Mr. Player has given me, I can feel the muscles working. But as soon as I sing I can't seem to make them work any more. I go straight back to singing from my throat."

"But you did have a loud singing voice when you were younger," Dad said. "I can remember you belting out things like *Happy Birthday* when you were little."

"Yes," Mum agreed. "I used to wonder where you kept that huge sound. You were only seven or eight. You must have been using your tummy muscles then. It couldn't have all come from your throat!"

Dad put his arms round Chloe and gave her a big

hug. "I wish I could wave a magic wand and help you," he said. "But I don't know anything about singing. I'm sure it'll come right in the end though."

"I did want to sing in the end-of-term concert," Chloe said sadly.

"You do as Mr. Player tells you," Mum advised. "I'm sure he knows best."

"And don't forget," Dad said, "we love you anyway, whatever happens."

It was good to know that her family was behind her. But as Saturday stretched into Sunday afternoon, a lead weight settled in Chloe's stomach. It was almost time to go back to school, and still there was no message from Pop or Lolly. Nothing would stop Chloe working towards her ambition, but it would be very hard to carry on cheerfully if she'd lost her two best school friends.

# 9 In Search of a Voice

It was so hard going back to Rockley Park not knowing what Pop and Lolly thought of her. Danny was as friendly as ever during the journey, but when they arrived Chloe chickened out of dropping her bag off at Paddock House. She didn't feel brave enough to face the girls yet. She stuck with Danny and they went into tea together.

"So what's going on?" he asked, chomping on a baguette. It had been obvious that Chloe hadn't wanted to talk in front of her parents in the car and so he was still in the dark about what was wrong.

She took a deep breath. "I can't sing at the concert because I can't make my voice loud enough," she said.

"Oh. Never mind." He took another mouthful. Splinters of crust and shreds of salad fell onto his plate. Chloe stared at him.

"Never mind! Is that all?" she demanded.

Danny shrugged. "You're in the right place to get all the help you need. What's the problem?"

Chloe couldn't believe it. Danny could be *so* dense sometimes.

"Rising Stars points, for a start!" she said.

"True," he acknowledged, nodding. "But there will be other concerts. And my drum teacher told me that teachers' decisions throughout the term are more important than the points awarded by the students at concerts. Anything else?" he asked, in his new capacity as problem solver. Chloe took a deep breath. Why was he being so irritating? He seemed determined to see her huge problem as a fuss about nothing.

"Only that I'm a failure and so Pop and Lolly probably won't want to be friends with me any more." Chloe hated the way she was sounding so pathetic, but she was near to tears, and couldn't help her voice wobbling. Danny put the remains of his baguette down and looked at Chloe.

"Who'd want friends like that?" he asked. "*I* wouldn't."

Chloe tried to explain. "That's all very well, but—"

"Here, let's ask them," he butted in. "Hey, Pop! You wouldn't stop being friends with Chloe if she couldn't sing, would you?"

To Chloe's horror, Pop and Lolly were in the dining room, coming their way. Practically everyone in the room must have heard what Danny had said! Chloe rubbed her eyes furiously and tried to look as if she didn't care.

Pop banged her tray down on the table and plonked herself angrily into the chair opposite Chloe.

"Honestly! What a *horrible* thing to say, Danny!"

"What have *I* done?" Danny asked. "I was only—"

"Well, don't," said Lolly, putting her tray down quietly and sitting next to Chloe. "Can't you see she's upset?" She put her arm round Chloe and gave her a hug. "I'm *so* glad to see you," she said. "Pop and I have been worried sick."

Danny finished his tea, pushed back his chair and got up.

"Girls!" he muttered, and wandered off.

"We were at our house in Gloucestershire for the weekend," Pop told Chloe. "It's down in a valley. We can *never* get a signal for our mobiles there. It's so boring. So Lolly only got your text on the way back to school."

"That's why I only texted you back an hour ago," Lolly explained. "...And you didn't read the message, did you?" she added, seeing Chloe's face.

Chloe shook her head. "I switched my phone off and packed it in my bag this morning," she explained. "After not hearing from you over the weekend, I thought you definitely wouldn't text me today," she added awkwardly.

"And after what Tara said on Friday, we were afraid you'd disappear and we'd never see you again!" added Lolly. "You did mention not being able to use the right muscles for singing at the beginning of term, but we thought that had been fixed.

Is it still the same problem?"

Chloe told them all about it. It felt good unburdening herself to the twins. When she'd finished, Lolly gave her another hug.

"We didn't realize it was so serious," she told Chloe. "You poor thing, suffering all this time in silence. You should have said."

"I know," Chloe admitted sheepishly. "Jess told me off about that. And don't be cross with Danny for what he said. It's my fault. I really was scared that if I couldn't sing you might not want to be friends any more."

"Huh!" snorted Pop.

"Sorry," Chloe said in a small voice.

"Don't worry," Lolly said. "Some people really *are* like that."

"We liked you straight away because you were so ordinary," Pop told her.

Chloe couldn't help smiling. "Thanks!" she said.

"No, really!" said Pop. "You know what I mean. We meet so many people who only want to be friends because we're well known. We've got careful of going round with phoneys. They only let you down."

"Sometimes they're quite hard to spot," Lolly said. "So I'm not surprised you were wary of trusting us. But *we're* not phoneys, and we want to help. Tell us what to do and we'll do it!"

Chloe smiled a lopsided smile. If only it were that easy.

They finished their tea and went over to Paddock House. There was no sign of Tara.

"I saw her going over to the practice rooms as we arrived," Lolly said. "I don't think she went home at the weekend. Her parents are often abroad."

"We've got to get you singing somehow," Pop insisted. "I'm sure we can do it."

"But how?" asked Chloe. "Everything I've tried so far just makes it worse. I'm afraid I won't be able to stay here if I don't sort myself out soon." The twins had made Chloe feel so much better, she was beginning to think this fear was groundless too. But Lolly took it seriously.

"Has Mr. Player said anything like that?" Lolly asked. Chloe shook her head.

"No."

"I expect he doesn't want you to panic," Pop said.

"Don't worry," said Lolly. "You won't get thrown out in your first term. If it was near the end of the first *year* it might be a bit different." Chloe felt the fear come creeping back. Surely it wouldn't take *that* long to find the volume she needed!

"It's not as if you have to learn how to *sing*," mused Pop. "It's just that your voice is too quiet."

Chloe nodded sadly. "Yes, someone told me that even a baby can cry out loud without being taught and that it's my mind that's stopping me." Pop clutched Chloe's arm.

"That's it! You need something to get you to yell out loud without thinking. Maybe that would unlock your voice."

"Mmm," agreed Lolly. "That's not such a bad idea. Perhaps if someone gave you a fright you'd yell, and then you could turn the yell into a song."

"Do you think that might work?" Chloe looked at their anxious faces. "I'll give it a go," she added bravely. "As long as you don't give me a heart attack!"

"Lolly and I will plan something for you," Pop assured her in a spooky voice. "Prepare to be v-e-r-y scared!"

# 10 Alarms and Decisions

It wasn't long before a huge Christmas tree went up in the main hall. Some people had brought decorations from home, and hung them round the homework room to cheer it up. The whole atmosphere in the school was changing as the term galloped on towards Christmas. Everyone was getting more and more excited about the concert, and rehearsals were going on in every available practice room. Even Judge Jim's usually quiet courtyard often had someone there, trying a new riff on guitar, or singing the same phrase over and over again. It was difficult for the teachers of the usual school subjects to get the students to concentrate.

"There's more to chemistry than hair products!" Mrs.

Pinto complained one day when several boys wouldn't stop talking about which gel was best to produce seriously spiky hair for their performance.

Although Chloe was the only student in her year not taking part in the concert, she was just as jumpy as everyone else, but for a different reason. Pop and Lolly had enlisted everyone's help in their scheme to help Chloe find her voice, but far from helping, it was fast turning her into a nervous wreck.

The favourite ploy was jumping out at her, and Chloe was getting mighty tired of being ambushed everywhere she went. She took to spending time in the recording studio, where Mr. Timms wouldn't tolerate such behaviour. Although she wasn't allowed to do much, she loved just sitting in a corner and watching the vocalists, who stood alone in the small booth while they sang into the microphone. She could see what an important partnership it was between the performers and the engineer if a really good recording was to be made. But she couldn't stay in the recording studio all the time, and even going to bed wasn't safe... One evening Tara put a huge, black spider on Chloe's bed. Chloe didn't like spiders very much, though she wouldn't normally have been terrified. But as it set off at a canter over the duvet en route for Chloe's pillow, Pop let out a tremendous scream. She cowered in a corner pointing at Chloe's bed. Chloe assumed it was another trick and didn't take too much notice, but then Lolly started too.

"Ssspider. Chloe. *Spider!*" Lolly wasn't *that* good an actress. Chloe glanced down to see the thing just about to run over her hand. She jumped up in a panic, and the poor spider hurtled over the edge of the bed and dropped to the floor with an audible plop. Pop and Lolly took ages to calm down. They totally refused to go to bed until Mrs. Pinto had retrieved the poor creature from under the bed. The housemistress had to get down on her hands and knees and catch it with a postcard and a glass, while a giggling Chloe shone a torch so she could see what she was doing.

The next day, at lunch, Marmalade put a large black beetle on Chloe's tray while she wasn't looking. It ran out from under her napkin while she was carrying the tray, and her nerves were so jangled she dropped the lot!

"It's no good," Danny said, once everyone had helped clear up the mess and they were sitting down for their meal. "We're only making things worse. It's obvious that Chloe doesn't scream when she's frightened. We'll have to think of something else."

Chloe heaved a sigh of relief. It was good to know she wasn't going to be subjected to any more scares. But the problem with her voice hadn't gone away.

One afternoon, Chloe went to her favourite spot to try once again all the exercises and tips Mr. Player had recommended. Although lots of people wandered beside the lake, hardly anyone bothered to walk round the far side. Here, sheltered by trees, she ran through everything he had taught her.

She relaxed her shoulders and neck, and imagined her tummy muscles pushing all the air out of her lungs. She pretended she had to sing to someone on the other side of the water, and for a moment her voice did seem to carry a bit further. Then it faltered, along with her confidence, and she could tell that not even the ducks swimming near the shore were impressed.

Ankle deep in crunchy, winter leaves, Chloe stared out over the lake. Rockley Park School looked lovely in the thin sunlight. She could imagine how the house must have looked in days gone by. There would have been carriages rolling along the gravel drive, and ladies in long dresses walking with their friends and having tea on the lawn. Her heart was filled with affection for the place, and although she'd only been a pupil for a few weeks, the last thing she wanted was to leave.

She thought about what Mr. Watkins, her old music teacher, had said when her parents were worried about her career choice.

*"There are lots of career opportunities in the music industry. Singing is only a small part of it. There are many other things she could end up doing."*

Perhaps it was time she realized that what Judge Jim had told her was true. She *couldn't* always have everything she wanted. Maybe her voice would *never* work properly for her again.

She picked up a large chestnut leaf and twirled it in her fingers. Even if she *couldn't* sing, she still wanted to stay here. She was certain of that. The thought of returning to her old school and leaving this life behind was too awful to contemplate. Was there something else she might be good at? How about becoming a recording engineer? She found the technical side of things really interesting.

Chloe dropped the leaf and sighed. It would be very hard recording other singers when she wanted to be one herself. She didn't know what the future might bring, but she knew that she wouldn't give up on singing. Chloe could never, ever do that. She would *always* hope. And as she headed back to Paddock House, Chloe was at least sure of one thing. She had wonderful friends, who really cared about her, and that was worth an awful lot. Now she must be a generous friend to them, and try not to be jealous when they were able to perform at the concert, and she wasn't.

# 11 Making the Best of It

"Well, I've done *everything* Mr. Player has taught me this term and I *still* can't sing out loud," Chloe announced.

Lolly, who was sitting on her bed, reading, flopped back with a huge sigh. "Well, you've done all you can for now, Chloe. I'm sure you'll get points from Mr. Player for determination and dedication even if you don't get any for actually performing. He couldn't ask for a more hard-working student. I wish I was as brave as you."

"You don't have anything to be brave about," Chloe said. "Your life is perfect."

"Is that what you think?" said Lolly. She ignored Chloe's surprised expression and changed the subject.

"Come and tell me what you think of this." She opened her wardrobe and took out a dress in dreamy shades of green and blue.

"It's gorgeous!" Chloe held it up admiringly.

"I brought it from home for my performance. Pop has one the same in reds and yellows."

"I've never seen anything like it!" Chloe said, letting the silky fabric run through her hands.

"Just as well Mummy is rich," sniffed Tara from the doorway. Pop followed her into the room, and poked her in the back.

"Actually," said Pop, "we earned these. We were supposed to be paid for modelling them but we asked if we could have the dresses instead."

"It was a freezing day in the middle of winter and we had to wear them on the beach in Brighton," Lolly said. "It was for a summer feature in a magazine, but they always do them months in advance. I was so cold I thought my nose was going to drop off!"

"Remember how we kept slipping on the pebbles in those silly shoes we had to wear?" Pop reminded her.

"You fell over and got a mark on your dress. Everyone was furious."

"So was I," Lolly said. "I got a terrible bruise on my bum!"

"What are you wearing for the concert, Tara?" asked Pop.

"Black, of course," she replied.

"Don't you ever get a bit, well, tired of black?" said Lolly. "I know it's really sophisticated and everything, but...all the time?"

The thought struck Chloe that Tara looked a bit like the spider she'd put on Chloe's bed. She was all spindly arms and legs, and her black mohair jumper gave her quite a spidery body. It was hard not to giggle.

Tara smoothed her hands down her skintight black jeans and scowled. "Black suits my personality," she said.

Pop snorted. "That's true!"

"How are your rehearsals going?" Lolly asked, ignoring her sister. "You're playing with Danny, aren't you?"

Tara glared at Pop for a moment before she replied. "I'm perfect," she boasted. "But Danny isn't practising enough. We need to work together more but I can never get him to agree when." Chloe couldn't believe *that* for a moment. Danny *lived* for his drums. If he wasn't meeting Tara to practise, then there must be a good reason.

Chloe tried hard not to let the thought enter her mind, but she found herself not wanting Tara to do well at the concert. In fact, it wasn't only Tara. To have unkind thoughts about her would be understandable, but a small part of Chloe wanted *everyone* to perform badly. She kept telling herself not to feel this way, but the hope kept creeping into her mind. If *she* couldn't perform at all, why should anyone else do brilliantly? Better still, why couldn't something happen to get the concert cancelled entirely? It wasn't very nice having these thoughts. She was jealous, plain and simple. It was horrible, but true.

"It's funny how so many rock musicians wear black," said Pop, gazing at Tara. "Or if not black they often wear really scruffy clothes, as if they don't care *what* they look like."

"It's because we rock musicians care about the music, unlike you *pop* singers," sneered Tara.

"We care about the music *and* what we look like," Pop argued. "The whole act is important."

"Oh, come on. Don't let's argue," begged Lolly. "Can't you two agree to differ about pop and rock music? After all, it's all *music.*"

"Huh!" said Tara darkly. "Are you sure about that?"

Lolly put her hands over her ears. "No more!" she yelled. "If I hear this argument again, I'll *scream.*"

"You can be a rock chick as long as we're allowed to be pop divas," Chloe said.

Tara looked at her and laughed. "*You're* not likely to be *either*!" she began, but Pop picked up a pillow from her bed and flung it at her. Lolly and Chloe scrambled to rescue the dress and get out of the way as Tara and Pop started bopping each other in earnest.

"Sometimes, I think Pop and Tara are more like twins than Pop and me!" said Lolly. "Look at them.

They're really enjoying themselves!"

It was true. They were giggling like mad in between bopping each other with pillows.

"But Pop is much nicer than Tara," Chloe whispered, wincing as Pop fell off the bed, arms flailing.

"Yes, but Tara is nicer when she forgets about putting on an act," Lolly replied. "It's a shame she hasn't got any brothers or sisters to sort her out."

Chloe looked at Tara, who was helping Pop up. Lolly was right. She *was* nicer when she wasn't putting on an act. She even *looked* better. Her usually pale face was flushed a healthy pink, and her eyes, so often dark and unhappy-looking, were sparkling with fun.

"What *have* you been doing?" Rosie, an older girl who was the prefect on their corridor, put her head round their door.

"Pillow fight," said Pop with satisfaction. "Why?"

Rosie shook her head in disbelief. "It's just that I've never seen a famous model look such a mess before," she said. Chloe laughed. Rosie was so right. Pop's T-shirt was all crumpled and pulled askew, and her hair, instead of being sleek and shiny, was full of tangles.

"There's a message for you, Chloe," Rosie continued. "Could you go to the recording studio please? Mr. Timms wants to see you."

"Mr. Timms? What does he want?" asked Chloe.

"*I* don't know," Rosie told her. "But he said to go right away. You'd better hurry and find out!"

"Chloe Tompkins, in trouble again!" said Tara. Pop gave her an extra-hard bop with her pillow and she collapsed onto the bed.

Chloe and Lolly exchanged glances. "Of *course* you're not in trouble, Chloe," Lolly said confidently. "Are you?"

"No! I don't think so," said Chloe. "But I'd better go and find out what he wants."

Mr. Timms wasn't the sort of person you kept waiting, and Chloe didn't want to get on the wrong side of such an important teacher. She zipped up her fleece and hurried out of the room. What could Mr. Timms want?

# 12 Danny's Good Turn

Chloe raced over to the main house. Why *did* Mr. Timms want to see her? She'd coiled up some cables yesterday and put them away. Had she done it badly? Perhaps she'd put them in the wrong place and he couldn't find them!

She sped downstairs as quickly as she could, into the basement of the building. The red light outside the studio wasn't lit, so she knew it was all right to go in. Mr. Timms was making himself a drink in the tiny kitchen.

"Ah! Chloe. Just the person I..." His voice trailed away. He was so vague when he wasn't actually working. "Was it you who coiled this...?"

Oh no! She must have made a mistake, though the cable he was pointing to, hanging up where she'd left it, *looked* okay. Chloe swallowed nervously.

"Yes," she admitted.

"Very good," he said. "Very neat." After a few moments, he added, "I like neat..." He waved her out of the way and went through to the control room with his tea. Chloe followed, feeling a bit better. You just had to be patient with Mr. Timms.

"You want to record..." Mr. Timms waved his hand vaguely, "...Danny?"

"Danny?"

"Yes. He wants to do a demo... Said you might want..."

"Hi, Chloe!" It was Danny's voice, coming out of one of the speakers, and it made Chloe jump. He must be somewhere in the studio! She looked through the large, soundproofed window that separated the control room from the larger of the two recording rooms, and her friend waved at her cheerfully. He'd been sorting out the drum kit.

"Thanks for coming. I need to make a recording for Tara and I thought you might want to help. Hang on, I'll come through." In a moment, he was in the control room. "Mr. Timms said you could give me a hand if you like," he explained when they were together.

"Really?" Chloe's eyes shone. "You mean it?" She looked from Danny to Mr. Timms and back again.

"If you don't mess about," Mr. Timms said. "And do as you're... Let's get on then..."

Chloe couldn't believe it. This was brilliant! She was going to be part of a real recording! Danny led the way back to the drum kit, and Mr. Timms showed them how to position the five drum microphones.

"We need that mic stand over there." She picked up the black metal stand Mr. Timms was pointing at and carried it carefully to him. "Put it so the microphone on it is angled over the floor tom." Danny pointed to the large drum next to his bass drum and Chloe set the stand down. "You'll need to make it lower," said Mr. Timms.

"Like that?"

"Bit more. That's it. Now, clip this mic onto the snare drum."

"What's this called?" Chloe asked Danny, pointing to a funny pair of cymbals with a little gap between them. They were on a tall, silver stand and were attached to a pedal on the floor.

"That's a high hat," Danny told her. "Look." He pressed the pedal with his foot and the top cymbal closed down onto the bottom one with a satisfying little *Tchk!* When he took his foot off the pedal, the cymbal went back up again.

"I don't know how you manage to do so many different things at the same time," she told Danny, gazing at all the equipment. "It's like rubbing your tummy and patting your head at the same time, only more difficult!"

When all the microphones had been positioned correctly, Mr. Timms and Chloe went through to the control room, leaving Danny to get settled at his drums.

"Here are your five mics on the screen," he showed Chloe, pointing to the lines on a nearby monitor. "Put these round your neck; you'll need them in a bit." He handed her some headphones. Everyone called headphones "cans" in the recording studio.

"You can speak to Danny via this mic here on the mixing desk. Get him to play the bass drum first while you set up the sound level for it."

Chloe felt very important sitting at the mixing desk with all its dozens of knobs. She leaned over to speak into the mic.

"Give me some bass, please," she said, like she'd heard Mr. Timms say to people.

"Okay," Danny said. She could hear him perfectly. He thumped away with his bass pedal and one of the lines on the monitor jumped up and down. Mr. Timms showed Chloe how to set it at the correct level. When it was about right, she asked Danny to stop and play his snare drum instead. When all the recording levels had been set, Mr. Timms told her to get Danny to do a run-through. Danny twirled a drumstick at her through the glass partition and set off. She sat back to watch him. She felt like a real professional.

"Watch the levels, Chloe," Mr. Timms warned, tapping the monitor. "Look at the cymbals. They're going to drown out the rest if you don't tweak it a bit." Oops! Perhaps it wasn't as easy as she'd thought!

It didn't take long to record the piece Danny wanted to perform. When it was done he came into the control room and they all listened to the playback.

"What do you think?" asked Mr. Timms. Chloe tried hard to think of something that would improve the recording.

"Is the snare drum a bit quiet?" she asked.

Mr. Timms nodded. "You could increase it a bit if you like." He showed her which knob to turn, and she adjusted it until the sound was more balanced.

"That's fine!" said Danny when they'd played it back again. "Thanks. Tara *will* be pleased."

Mr. Timms took a tape out of a tape machine and handed it to Chloe.

"Put your name on this tape," he told her. "This is your first recording as a sound engineer. It's important to keep a record of your work." Chloe was speechless with delight. She held onto the tape as if it were the most precious thing in the world.

"This is Tara's copy," Mr. Timms added, handing another tape to Danny. "You can tell her she's to bring it back after the concert to be used again. I don't approve of waste. Well, go on then," he said. "Well done. Off you go. I've got better things to do... When I was at Abbey Road I didn't..."

Danny and Chloe scooted out of his way and back into the main hall.

"Thanks for helping," Danny said.

"No! Thank *you*!" Chloe said. "I've had a brilliant time. You didn't really need me though, did you? Mr. Timms could have done that recording in his sleep. What made you think of me?"

Danny shrugged. "Do you mind giving the tape to Tara?" he said, not meeting Chloe's eyes and changing the subject. "Only she's such a pain about rehearsing. She's so bossy, always thinking she knows best. If she has the tape, she can practise without me there. Then

I might just manage the performance without losing my cool!"

"Of course I will, but Danny, why..."

He hurriedly thrust the tape at her, still avoiding her eyes. "No reason," he said, and then relented. "Well, I thought, you know..." He shrugged. "You've had a hard time, and you really like the recording studio..." He looked at her at last, and blushed.

"You're beginning to sound like Mr. Timms," she complained. Then she found she was blushing too.

# 13 An Awful Fright

It was the last day of term and the day of the concert. Loads of parents were arriving. Straight after the concert, everyone would be heading home for Christmas, but no one could get excited about that until the performances were safely over. No one except Chloe, that is.

Chloe was so looking forward to seeing her parents, and her little brother too. She couldn't wait for Pop and Lolly to meet Ben at last. She'd told them so much about him. At the same time, he was too young to worry about her lack of progress with singing. He, alone of all the people she knew, wouldn't be asking how she'd got on this term. With Ben, Chloe could be herself, and forget her worries, and she badly needed to be able to do that.

She had plenty of time to pack her bags while everyone else was frantically rehearsing.

"I'll strip your beds if you like," she volunteered to Pop and Lolly, after Mrs. Pinto had asked everyone to put their bedding in piles to help the domestic staff. "I'll do yours as well, if you like," she offered to Tara.

"Thanks!" said Tara, looking very surprised. "That would be great."

Chloe was glad to have something to do. It was horrible watching everyone get ready for the concert. She couldn't stop herself being jealous, however hard she tried, so helping out was a way of making her feel less guilty.

She had asked her parents to come after the concert was over. It was going to be hard enough sitting in the audience watching all her friends perform, without her parents feeling sorry for her as well. The last thing she wanted was to cry, and she was afraid she might if they were with her.

Chloe took her recent recording out of a drawer and

put it on top of her bag so she could show her parents when they arrived. That was one really good thing that had happened. She would be able to say that she had achieved *something* even if it was nothing to do with her singing.

Just then, Pop and Lolly burst into the room.

"Guess what? Mrs. Pinto wants to take a photo of us all outside Paddock House. We're going to put our dresses on!" Pop whizzed to her wardrobe and pulled out her stunning dress.

"You too, Chloe," urged Lolly, slipping her dress over her head. "This is a house photo. You're just as important as anyone."

"What should I wear?" Chloe asked.

"It doesn't matter," Pop assured her.

"No, really. It doesn't," said Tara disagreeably, leaning against the doorway.

"Are you coming in or are you just going to stand there, being horrible?" demanded Pop.

"Actually," Tara replied, "I came to give Chloe a message."

## An Awful Fright

"Oh!" Chloe remembered. "I'm supposed to be on car-park duty."

"It's not about that," Tara said. "The message is from Danny. I saw him just now in the main hall. He said he'd seen your little brother wandering around outside on his own." Chloe jumped to her feet.

"Ben? What's he doing here? Mum and Dad aren't coming until after the concert. I told them not to."

Pop and Lolly exchanged glances. "Danny knows your little brother though, doesn't he, Chloe? Surely he wouldn't make a mistake?" said Pop.

"Perhaps your parents have got here early," Lolly suggested.

"But I was sure Mum knew I didn't want them to come early! Where *is* Ben?" Chloe asked Tara. "Did Danny grab him?"

Tara shook her head. "I don't know. I didn't see any annoying toddlers," she said. "There were too many cars and people about. It's mad down there at the moment."

"Oh no! Ben's terrible at running off," said Chloe

anxiously. "He could get lost, or hurt." A vision of Ben being knocked down and injured flashed through her mind. It was too horrible to contemplate. She had to go and find him.

"We'll help!" said Pop. But Chloe had already gone. She pushed past Tara and raced down the corridor. Mum and Dad wouldn't have let Ben wander off on his own. But sometimes he could be so difficult to hang on to. He could have wriggled through the crowd of parents and be anywhere.

Chloe hurried over to the main house. The large hall was full of students and parents, all chattering excitedly. There were so many people that lunch was going to be in three sittings. The first lot, seniors and their families, were already going in. Chloe couldn't see Ben, Danny or her mum and dad anywhere. She pushed her way against the tide of people and out of the front door. Cars were all over the place. Some were parked, and others were arriving. People were everywhere, but there was still no sign of her little brother.

"Chloe!" It was Marmalade. She grabbed his arm. "Have you seen him?"

"I've been looking for you," Marmalade said. "Danny saw your brother."

"Where?" She scanned the car park wildly.

"He was heading for the lake! Danny's gone after him."

Chloe didn't wait to hear any more. Her heart was in her mouth. She ran towards the lake as fast as she could.

"Chloe, wait!"

If only she'd been wearing her trainers instead of her best shoes in honour of the concert. She slipped and slid on the gravel as she wove her way between people. It was better on the grass. She paused for a moment to kick off her shoes, and then she carried on running. She could see Danny down by the lake but she couldn't see Ben.

"Please let him be all right," she panted. "Please let him. Don't let him drown."

Danny glanced up and saw her. He waved and bent

down to the surface of the water. Chloe could hear people behind her, running to catch her up. But all she could think about was her baby brother. She stumbled on a tussocky clump of grass and almost fell. As she recovered herself she heard a loud splash.

"NO!" she screamed. "NO! SAVE HIM, DANNY! SAVE HIM!"

# 14 What Friends Are For

Chloe splashed into the shallows and sank ankle deep into the soft mud at the bottom. She couldn't stop screaming. "BEN! BEN!" Why wasn't Danny saving him?

Then he splashed in to join her. She was still screaming. She didn't feel the icy water. She was thrashing about, searching for her little brother but she couldn't see anything in the mud she was stirring up. Danny reached her and grabbed her arms.

"Don't go any further, it's dangerous!" he yelled. Marmalade was there too and together the boys dragged her out onto the bank. She was still screaming, totally out of control. What use was fame or money or anything else if her little brother had drowned?

Pop and Lolly were waiting on the bank. They were shouting too.

"He's all right, Chloe! Really! Listen to us. He's all right!" Pop threw her arms round Chloe and held her tight, as Danny and Marmalade let go. Tears were streaming down Chloe's cheeks and Lolly did her best to wipe them away.

"Where is he?" Chloe broke free of Pop and spun round, desperate to catch sight of her brother.

"Please, Chloe," begged Danny, his teeth chattering with cold. "Calm down. It's all right. He's quite safe."

"*But where is he?*" she yelled.

Lolly took Chloe's face in her hands and held it until their eyes met.

"Ben is safe," she said quietly, and Chloe knew that what Lolly said must be true.

"Where is he?" Chloe begged again, her voice ragged.

"With your mum and dad, I expect. On his way here in your car," said Pop. Chloe stared at her, and then at the rest of them. She couldn't make sense of it. What was going on? Her whole body was shaking as if there had been a terrible tragedy. Had there been or not? What were they all doing at the lake if Ben was in a car?

"I don't understand," Chloe said, her voice trembling. Her friends exchanged glances. No one knew what to say.

"Please don't be angry," Lolly begged, shivering in her thin dress. "We were trying to help you get your voice back. We hoped if you were scared enough you might get all worked up and then shout at us when you realized it was a trick."

"And it worked!" Pop said. "I've never heard anyone scream as loudly as you did just now. You *have* got your voice back!"

"We didn't mean it to work quite this well, though," Danny said anxiously. "We didn't think you'd throw yourself into the water to save him."

"Why *not*?" Chloe yelled, sudden relief giving way to fury. *"He's my little brother and I was scared!"*

Danny ducked as her flailing arms nearly hit him.

"I'm sorry," he begged, ducking another blow. "It was all I could think of to help you find your voice. We thought you'd shout because you were angry at the trick, not because you really thought Ben was in danger."

Chloe took a deep, shuddering breath. "Of course I didn't realize it was a trick," she said, her voice wobbling. "He's only little, and I thought he might drown..." Her voice trailed off, and she began to sob in earnest.

Lolly and Pop put their arms round her. Danny looked to Marmalade for help.

"Don't cry, Chloe," Marmalade told her, trying to sound upbeat. "He really *is* all right. We're all sorry we frightened you so much, but it did work. You *have* found your voice."

"I'm sure you'll be able to sing at the next concert," Danny added.

Pop let go of Chloe in a panic.

"The concert!" she gasped.

Lolly ignored her sister. She gave Chloe another hug

and then took hold of her arm. "Come on," she urged. "You're frozen and you've had a bad fright. Let's get you back to Paddock House so you can change."

Chloe's friends were chilled to the bone as well. Pop and Lolly's dresses seemed intact but even though they weren't torn, they had been splashed horribly with muddy water. The gauzy fabric hung in rags, the jewel colours dulled. And their delicate shoes looked ruined. Marmalade and Danny were as soaked as Chloe with the battle they'd had to drag her out of the lake. Long strings of green weed slimed all over their sodden jeans, and their trainers would never be the same again.

Chloe's heart was still thumping with the fright she'd had but, slowly, her fury at her friends for tricking her was giving way to relief that Ben really was safe. Her anger faded even more as she realized why they'd done it. Even though their trick had got out of control, they'd done it all for her. And on this, of all days, when they needed to be thinking about the concert.

"Thank you," she said quietly. Then she remembered,

and sang it for them. "Thank YOU!" Her voice soared. The sound poured out of her lungs, pure and sustained. She could feel the power deep inside her. This was what she had lost and her friends had helped her find. She looked at their pale faces; they were all still watching her with such worried expressions.

"Well, go on!" she urged them, relief making her almost gleeful. "You'd better go and get ready, hadn't you? Your parents will be waiting for their lunch, and then it's the concert!"

# 15 Chloe's Voice

Back at school, they all parted company. Everyone needed hot showers and dry clothes, but even though she was dripping wet Chloe wanted to tell someone her news. She pushed her way through the crush of parents, students and teachers in the main hall. There he was, Judge Jim Henson, talking to an elderly woman who looked very elegant in bright clothes and matching headdress. He caught sight of Chloe and raised his eyebrows. She must have looked a strange sight in her dripping clothes.

"I've got my voice back!" she told him happily. "I can sing again!"

Judge Jim's face lit up and he nodded slowly.

He smiled at his companion and said, "This here is young Chloe Tompkins, Joan. She is either up or down this child. There's nothing in between. Just now, as you can see, she's up. Joan is a singer too, Chloe. She's been singing for more years than you can imagine."

"Why Jim, that's not very complimentary for a lady," Joan teased him. Judge Jim just smiled, crinkling his face into even more wrinkles. "Pleased to meet you, Chloe," Joan went on, holding her hand out for Chloe to shake. "It looks as if you've been celebrating finding your voice by having a Christmas swim!"

"Not quite," Chloe said. "But I ought to go and get changed."

"Well done with that voice," Judge Jim said with a smile, offering his hand. She took it. But that didn't seem enough. She was so happy, and she didn't want him to think she hadn't appreciated his advice, even though she hadn't been any good at taking it.

"Thank you!" she said, and found herself giving him a big hug. At first he seemed surprised, and she wondered if she'd done the right thing. Then he hugged her back, and she could hear his big, booming laugh echo through his chest.

Chloe hurried back to her room. Pop and Lolly had just showered and were drying their hair.

"How are your dresses?" Chloe asked anxiously.

"We rinsed them out and Mrs. Pinto is tumble drying them," Pop said. "She's keeping an eye on them. They should be all right if they don't get too hot."

"The seams might not dry in time," added Lolly. "But it won't matter. We can wear them a bit damp. How's your voice?"

Chloe gathered her breath and powered up through a scale with the sort of volume Mr. Player had been asking her for all term. Pop shook her damp hair.

"That is one truly awesome voice," she said. "I can't believe you've had that amazing sound locked away for so long!"

"Great," said Tara, lounging on her bed. "There'll be no peace in this room now." But even she was smiling slightly.

# Rising Star

Time was ticking on. After a quick shower, Chloe took the twins' shoes into the bathroom and did her best to clean them up. They wouldn't look too bad onstage, she decided, but they looked pretty awful close up. You couldn't expect to tramp around the muddy margins of a lake in diamanté sandals and expect them to stay as good as new. She hoped Pop and Lolly's mother wouldn't be too angry.

Everyone was having lunch with their parents except for Chloe, Tara and Danny, so they sat together.

"How's your voice?" Danny asked, as they wolfed down their lasagne.

"Don't encourage her!" warned Tara.

"Sorry."

Chloe laughed. "It's fine. I feel really confident. Thanks, Danny." He met her eyes and they grinned at each other. With the concert starting in a few minutes, the atmosphere in the dining hall was fizzing. If Tara hadn't been with them Chloe might even have given Danny a hug!

"Look! There's Mr. Player," she said instead. "I must

go and tell him." She went over to where he was queuing for his lunch. "It's back!" Chloe told him excitedly. He knew what she meant straight away.

"Oh, well done!" he said. "What was it? The throwing-up exercise, or calmly leaving it alone to recover on its own?"

"Neither!" said Chloe. "It was my friends."

"Oh? Well, I'm very pleased for you. Don't let it disappear again, will you? I have some great songs for you to learn next term. You're going to have to work really hard to catch up, but I know you can do it."

All the students, parents and teachers were assembling in the theatre. The backstage area wasn't used for Rising Star concerts. The performers all sat at the front, where it was only a few steps up onto the stage. This way, everyone could enjoy the concert, and perform and vote as well. Each person had a programme and a pen to mark each act out of ten. Over the holiday, the staff would analyse the results, and when the students came back they would see which performance had been awarded the most Rising Star points.

Even though Chloe was not performing, she had been allowed to sit with her friends down at the front. Danny glanced at her, and she could see he was thinking the same thing.

"I can't believe I'm here," he said.

"Me too," she agreed. "Even though I'm not a part of the concert this time, I'm here at Rockley Park, learning to be a pop singer. And now I've found my voice, next term's going to be amazing!"

"I know," Danny said. "I'm going to be drumming in front of an audience for the first time in my life!"

"Oh, come on," said Tara. "Don't go all soft on me, Danny. I hope you're not going to let me down. Are you sure you know your part properly?" Danny said nothing, but he smiled slightly at Chloe and she grinned back.

Pop and Lolly were first up. Onstage, the lights made them look impossibly gorgeous. They strutted their stuff like the catwalk queens they were, singing as if their lives depended on it. Chloe gave them both nine out of ten.

She crossed her fingers for Danny's act, but he didn't need it. His drumming was fantastic. She did *try* not to be biased, but she gave him ten anyway. To Chloe's surprise, Tara was very nervous and made several mistakes on guitar. She sang well enough, though, and Chloe gave her seven.

Listening to the buzz of conversation in the hall during the interval, it seemed Danny might be favourite so far out of the year sevens.

"Of course it doesn't mean anything," said Tara. "This is only the first concert. There are *two* next term, and two more the term after that. Anything could happen before the end of the year." That was true. Even Chloe would have a chance to catch up. But it was a typical Tara remark.

They were just about to go back in for the second half of the concert when a car drew up. It was Chloe's family. As soon as the car stopped she raced over and opened the back door. Ben held out his arms to her, grinning all over his face. Tears filled Chloe's eyes. She undid his seat belt and lifted him out. She hugged him so tight he wriggled to get down, but she kept a tight grip on his hand.

"My voice is back!" she told her parents triumphantly.

"Well done!" her dad said. "I knew you could do it."

Chloe beamed at them all. She was glad about everything. Her brother was safe, her voice was back, she had loads of good friends, and next term she would be up there onstage, singing her heart out – ready to be a Rising Star!

# ✳ So you want to be a pop star?

✳

Turn the page to read some top tips on how to make your dreams
✳ come true... ✳
✳

# ✳ Making it in the music biz ✳

Think you've got tons of talent?
Well, music maestro Judge Jim Henson,
Head of Rock at top talent academy Rockley
Park, has put together his hot tips to help
you become a superstar...

✳ Number One Rule: Be positive!
You've got to believe in yourself.

✳ Be active! Join your school choir
or form your own band.

✳ Be different! Don't be afraid to stand
out from the crowd.

✳ Be determined! Work hard and stay focused.

✳ Be creative! Try writing your own material –
it will say something unique about you.

✳ Be patient! Don't give up if things
don't happen overnight.

✳ Be ready to seize opportunities
when they come along.

✳ Be versatile! Don't have a one-track mind – try out new things and gain as many skills as you can.

✳ Be passionate! Don't be afraid to show some emotion in your performance.

✳ Be sure to watch, listen and learn all the time.

✳ Be willing to help others. You'll learn more that way.

✳ Be smart! Don't neglect your school work.

✳ Be cool and don't get big-headed! Everyone needs friends, so don't leave them behind.

✳ Always stay true to yourself.

✳ And finally, and most importantly, enjoy what you do!

Go for it! It's all up to you now...

# Usborne Quicklinks

For links to exciting websites where you can find out more about becoming a pop star and even practise your singing with online karaoke, go to the Usborne Quicklinks Website at www.usborne-quicklinks.com and enter the keywords "fame school".

# Internet safety

When using the Internet make sure you follow these safety guidelines:

✴ Ask an adult's permission before using the Internet.

✴ Never give out personal information, such as your name, address or telephone number.

✴ If a website asks you to type in your name or email address, check with an adult first.

✴ If you receive an email from someone you don't know, do not reply to it.

For another fix of

read

Secret Ambition

#  1 What's Wrong?

Pop 'n' Lolly, the famous Lowther twins, strutted along the catwalk behind the supermodel Tikki Deacon. All three were wearing exotic, designer dresses, with long, jewel-coloured chiffon scarves. The disco music accompanying them roared out in a deafening blast that seemed to push them along, pace for pace in time with the music.

As Tikki reached the end of the walk, she turned abruptly and sashayed past the twins, the silk of her dress flowing round her ankles like ruffled water. Pop turned too, but something was wrong with her identical twin. Lolly had stopped, and was staring blindly into the lights as if transfixed. Pop turned again towards her sister, never missing a beat. Perfectly in time with the music, she grabbed Lolly's arm and yanked her round. Keeping a firm hold, Pop marched Lolly back up the catwalk, moving from the hips in the unmistakable model shimmy that they had practised so much. Amused laughter and then loud applause saw them through the curtain to backstage.

"What on *earth* do you think you were doing?" demanded Tikki, glaring at them angrily. Tikki Deacon was almost as famous for her quick temper as she was for her fabulous looks and jet-setting lifestyle. "How dare you try to upstage me like that!" she said. "You were supposed to turn and come straight off, not dawdle at the end like a couple of idiots! Who do you think you are?"

"Sorry," said Pop. "I think maybe Lolly's coming down with flu or something."

"Well, keep her away from me then!" Tikki snapped, backing into a rail of dresses. "I'm doing a fashion shoot in Acapulco on Tuesday and I don't want to miss it."

Lolly had already gone into the tiny corner reserved for the twins, and had begun to get changed. Backstage was chaotic, with hardly room to move. There were models everywhere, and dressers scrambling to take the precious clothes as soon as they had been discarded. Pop wormed her way through the crowd to Lolly and flung off her gorgeous dress in a fury.

"You nearly ruined *everything*," she hissed. "If we're not careful Tikki will refuse to work with us, and the designer won't have us back again." She threw the dress and scarf into the arms of a waiting dresser and scrambled into her jeans and jacket. "What's the matter with you?" she demanded. "You're not usually such a dreamer."

"Sorry," apologized Lolly. "I'm not really coming down with flu."

"I know *that*," said Pop, "it was just the first excuse I could think of."

The girls made their way to the foyer of the hotel, where their mother was waiting for them, along with their agent, Satin Fountain-Blowers.

"Wonderful as always, darlings," said their mum. She went to kiss them and then pulled away. "I do wish you'd take that make-up off though."

"We'll do it later," said Pop. "Can we go straight home?"

Satin nodded. "The taxi's waiting," she told them. "I know you're in a hurry to get to school for the beginning of the new term. Are you all right?" she added. Satin was very quick to pick up on their moods. She had been the twins' agent for years, ever since their mother had sent a photograph of them to Satin's agency when Pop and Lolly were really little. Satin had found the twins lots of modelling jobs, but today had been special, even for the famous twins. Working with the supermodel Tikki Deacon was a fantastic chance to raise their profile even higher, but any problems would reflect badly on Satin as well as the twins.

To find out what happens next read

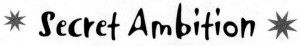 **Secret Ambition**

**Cindy Jefferies'** varied career has included being a Venetian-mask maker and a video DJ. Cindy decided to write *Fame School* after experiencing the ups and downs of her children, who have all been involved in the music business. Her insight into the lives of wannabe pop stars and her own musical background means that Cindy knows how exciting and demanding the quest for fame and fortune can be.

Cindy lives on a farm in Gloucestershire, where the animal noises, roaring tractors and rehearsals of Stitch, her son's indie-rock band, all help her write!

To find out more about Cindy Jefferies, visit her website: www.cindyjefferies.co.uk